ZOG

By Julia Donaldson

Illustrated by Axel Scheffler

Scholastic Canada Ltd.

Toronto New York London Auckland Sydney
Mexico City New Delhi Hong Kong Buenos Aires

Madam Dragon ran a school, many moons ago.
She taught young dragons all the things
that dragons need to know.

Zog, the biggest dragon, was the keenest one by far.
He tried his hardest every day to win a golden star.

All the dragons in Year One were learning how to fly.
"High!" said Madam Dragon. "Way up in the sky!

"Now that you've been shown, you can practise on your own
And you'll all be expert flyers by the time you're fully grown."

Zog went off to practise,
flying fast and free.

He soared and swooped

and looped the loop . . .

then crashed into a tree.

Just then, a little girl came by. "Oh, please don't cry," she said.
"Perhaps you'd like a nice sticky Band-Aid for your head?"

"What a good idea!" said Zog. Then up and off he flew,
His Band-Aid gleaming pinkly as he zigzagged through the blue.

A year went by, and in Year Two
the dragons learned to roar.
"More!" said Madam Dragon.
"Louder, I implore!
Now that you've been shown,
you can practise on your own
And you'll all be champion roarers
by the time you're fully grown."

Zog went off to practise.

He roared with fearsome force.

He kept it up for hours on end . . .

but then his throat grew hoarse.

Just then the girl came by again. She said, "What rotten luck! Perhaps you'd like a nice soothing peppermint to suck?"

"What a good idea!" said Zog. Then up and off he flew,
And breathing fumes of peppermint he zigzagged through the blue.

A year went by, and in Year Three the dragons learned to blow.
"No!" said Madam Dragon. "Breathe out fire, not snow!
Now that you've been shown, you can practise on your own
And you'll all be breathing bonfires by the time you're fully grown."

Zog went off to practise.

He blew with all his might.

He twirled around in triumph . . .

and his wing tip caught alight.

Just then the girl came by again. She said, "You poor old thing. Perhaps you'd like a nice stretchy bandage for your wing?"

"What a good idea!" said Zog. Then up and off he flew,

His bandage flapping wildly as he zigzagged through the blue.

All the Year Four dragons were learning — can you guess?
"Yes!" said Madam Dragon. "How to capture a princess!

"Now that you've been shown, you can practise on your own.
You'll need to capture hundreds by the time you're fully grown."

Zog went off to practise.
 He tried and tried and tried,
But he simply couldn't manage.
 "I'm no good at this," he cried.

"I'll *never* win a golden star!"

Just then he saw the girl.

"Perhaps," she said, "you'd like to capture *me*?

I'm Princess Pearl."

"What a good idea!" said Zog.

Then up and off they flew,

The princess gripping tightly

as they zigzagged through the blue.

"Ah," said Madam Dragon. "Our first princess so far!
Congratulations, Zog, my dear; you've won a golden star!"

Zog was proud and happy,

and Pearl felt good as well.

She took the dragons' temperatures,

and nursed them when they fell.

A year went by and, in Year Five, the dragons learned to fight.

"Right!" said Madam Dragon. "Here comes a real live knight!"

Up spoke the knight: "My name," he said,
  "is Gadabout the Great.
I've come to rescue Princess Pearl.
  I hope I'm not too late."

Zog breathed fire and beat his wings.
"You can't! She's mine!" he roared.
"Oh, no, she's not!" yelled Gadabout,
and waved his trusty sword.

The other dragons crowded round
and watched them, all agog.
Who was going to win the fight,
Sir Gadabout or Zog?

Then Princess Pearl stepped forward, crying,
    "STOP, you silly chumps!
The world's already far too full of cuts and burns and bumps.
Don't rescue me! I won't go back to being a princess
And prancing round the palace in a silly frilly dress.

"I want to be a doctor, and travel here and there,
Listening to people's chests and giving them my care."

"Me, too!" exclaimed the knight, and took his helmet off his head.
"I'd rather wear a nice twisty stethoscope," he said.

"Perhaps, Princess, you'll train me up?" And Pearl replied, "Of course,
But I don't see how the two of us could fit upon your horse."

Then Zog said, "Flying doctors!
     I'd love to join the crew.
If you'll let me be your ambulance,
     then I can carry you."
"Bravo!" said Madam Dragon.
     "An excellent career!"
And all the Year Five dragons
     gave a loud resounding cheer.

Then Madam Dragon told the horse,
     "I really hope you'll stay.
I'll let you be my pupils' pet,
     and feed you lots of hay."

"What a good idea!" said Zog. Then up and off he flew,

The Flying Doctors waving as they zigzagged through the blue.

For Poppy – J.D.

For Gabriel and Raphael – A.S.

Scholastic Canada Ltd.
604 King Street West, Toronto, Ontario M5V 1E1, Canada

Scholastic Inc.
557 Broadway, New York, NY 10012, USA

Scholastic Australia Pty Limited
PO Box 579, Gosford, NSW 2250, Australia

Scholastic New Zealand Limited
Private Bag 94407, Botany, Manukau 2163, New Zealand

Scholastic Children's Books
Euston House, 24 Eversholt Street, London NW1 1DB, UK

www.scholastic.ca

Library and Archives Canada Cataloguing in Publication

Donaldson, Julia, author
Zog / by Julia Donaldson ; illustrated by Axel Scheffler.
Previously published: Scholastic, 2014.
ISBN 978-1-4431-5701-8 (paperback)
1. Readers (Primary). 2. Readers--Fantasy fiction.
I. Scheffler, Axel, illustrator II. Title.
PE1119.D663 2017   428.6   C2016-904692-3

6 5 4 3 2 1   Printed in Malaysia   108   17 18 19 20 21